The Princess and the Peach

Brown Watson
ENGLAND

First published 2016 by Brown Watson
The Old Mill, 76 Fleckney Road
Kibworth Beauchamp
Leicestershire LE8 0HG
ISBN: 978-0-7097-2321-9
© 2016 Brown Watson, England
Printed in Malaysia

Written by Lisa Regan
Illustrated by Angelika Scudamore

It was nearly Princess Tia's birthday, but the King had a problem.

What present could he give to a Princess who already has everything?

Princess Tia has heard about a precious peach. 'That's what I want most of all!' she pleads.

So the King sends a message. Anyone who can find the precious peach will win a million pounds!

Prince Paolo from Portugal gallops into town. 'Behold – a precious ring!' he declares.

The golden ring has an enormous diamond and six peach coloured stones.

But it isn't what Princess Tia wants. 'I already have so many rings,' she weeps.

A brave Nigerian knight gallops into town.
'Behold – a precious tiara!' he declares.

The tiara has many jewels and beautiful golden fruits all over it.

But it isn't what Princess Tia was hoping for. 'Tiaras hurt my head,' she says sadly.

A handsome duke from Denmark gallops into town. "Behold — a precious cloak!" he declares.

The cloak is soft and silky, with embroidered fruits made of gold thread.

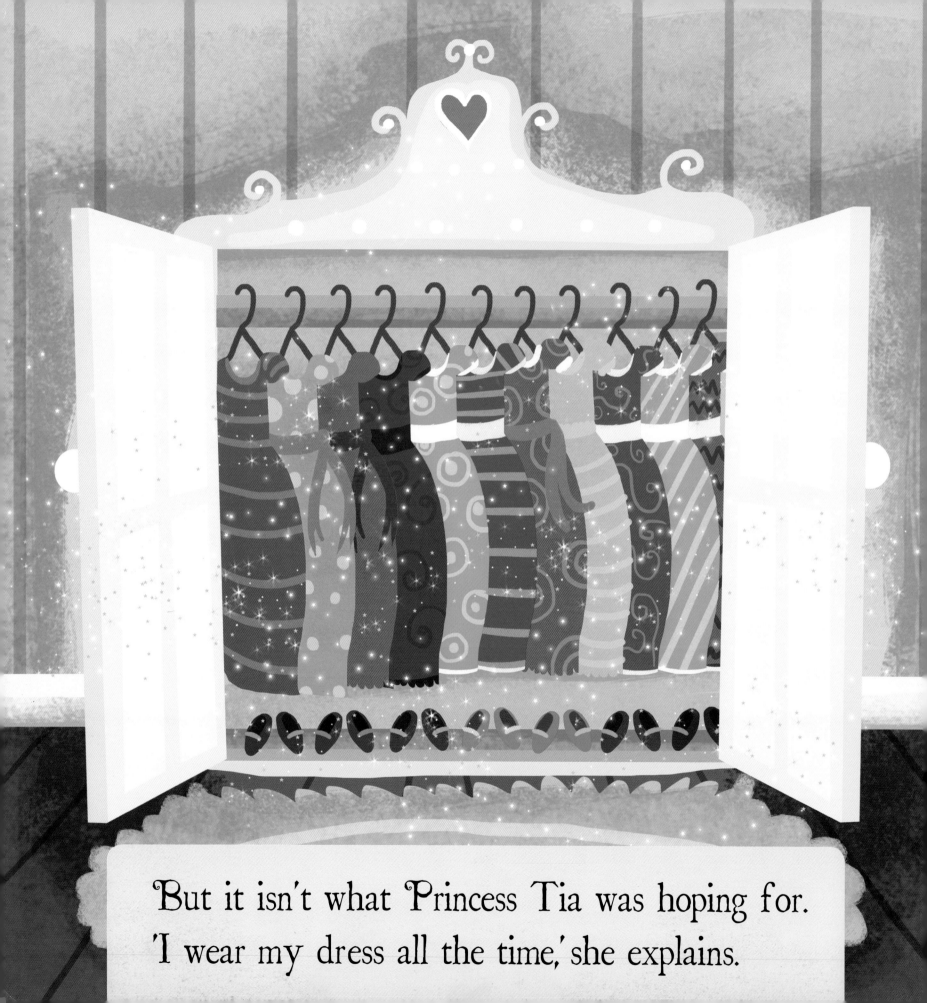

But it isn't what Princess Tia was hoping for.
'I wear my dress all the time,' she explains.

An enthusiastic count from Canada gallops into town. "Behold – a golden puppy!" he declares.

The puppy is simply adorable,
and licks the Princess's face.

But it isn't what Princess Tia was hoping for. 'Dog fur makes me sneeze,' she says sadly.

A heroic prince from the Middle East flies into town. "Behold – our finest foods!" he declares.

The Princess gazes at cakes and pastries and sweets spilling from the magic carpet.

But it isn't what Princess Tia was hoping for.
'My mummy won't let me eat all of those,' she sighs.

Princess Tia runs from the palace and into the town. A small boy sees her weeping.

He doesn't know she is a princess. 'Don't be sad,' he says. 'Here – eat this.'

The boy hands her a peach. It is delicious - juicy and sweet with golden flesh.

'This is it!' laughs Princess Tia. 'I have found my golden peach. It is just what I wanted!'